Five Gl

Addison Wesley Longman Limited
Edinburgh Gate, Harlow,
Essex CM20 2JE, England
and Associated Companies throughout the world.

ISBN 0-17-557023-X

This impression Longman Group Ltd 1995
Second impression 1998

Design by Shireen Nathoo Design

Cover illustration by Liz Pyle / Sharp Practice

Illustrations by Chris Daunt / Sharp Practice;
Mark Oldroyd / Arena; Liz Pyle / Sharp Practice

The Ghost by Richard Hughes is taken from *A Moment of Time*, published by Chatto and Windus.
We wish to thank The Society of Authors as the literary representative of the estate of W W Jacobs for permission to publish the simplified form of *Jerry Bundler*.

Produced through Longman Malaysia, PP

Contents

1

Not on the Passenger List

by Barry Pain

I could not sleep. The storm was very bad. The whole ship seemed alive with sounds. Everything seemed to move. The big case under my bed seemed very busy. I turned on the light and looked at it. It was moving slowly across the floor towards the door. Then a smaller case came out and stopped it on its way. I turned off the light again, and left them fighting and banging one another in the dark. At last I slept. I had a strange dream.

Daylight came, and I went to the bathroom to have a bath. The water was more than ready. It jumped out to meet me! After my bath I went back to my room. The steward brought me my morning tea. He told me the weather was getting better.

There were few people at breakfast that morning. But I wasn't the first. Mrs Derrison was coming out as I entered the restaurant. I thought she looked ill, but this did not surprise me. We said good morning. Then she said:

'I want to speak to you. Could we meet after breakfast?'

Mrs Derrison did not know much about travelling. She sometimes asked me about small things. I met her after breakfast. She was sitting in a chair, dressed in warm and expensive clothes. I could see now that she wasn't sea-sick.

'I didn't sleep all night,' she told me.

'I didn't have much sleep myself,' I said, 'but I had a strange dream.'

She looked out over the sea, and didn't seem to be listening. She was a woman of thirty-four or five, with an interesting face and fine eyes.

'Well,' I said, 'the wind is less strong now. We shall all sleep better tonight. Look, the sun's coming out at last. Now, Mrs Derrison, what's the trouble? How can I help you?'

'I don't think you can help me,' she answered sadly. She held out a hand in the sunlight. It looked small and thin, and it shook.

'I'm afraid,' she continued. 'I'm very much afraid.' I looked at her white face.

'But, Mrs Derrison, this doesn't make sense. We've had a bad storm, but it's nearly over, and this boat is as safe as a church. And we'll be in Liverpool the morning after next.'

'Yes, I know. It isn't the storm which makes me afraid. This is something quite different. And when I've told you, you'll think I'm not right in the head.'

'No, I shan't think that.'

'All right, I'll tell you. My husband Alec died three months ago. I'm going to England to marry another man.'

'I see. Please go on.'

'Alec died three months ago. But he's on this boat! I saw him last night. I think he's come for me!'

'Well,' I said, 'you know that's quite impossible, don't

you?'

'I thought that yesterday.'

'And you will tomorrow. Tell me what happened, and I will give you the explanation.'

'I went to my room at eleven last night. I turned on the light. He was sitting on the bed. I could see the side of his face. He wasn't looking at me. The light shone on his head. He was wearing a blue dressing gown and red shoes. That's what he always wore. There was something heavy in the pocket of his dressing gown. Then I remembered something he once told me. When he was travelling he always put his watch, money and keys there at night. As I looked, he turned his head towards me. It came round very slowly. Till then I was surprised but not afraid. But when the head turned round, I got really afraid. You see, it was Alec – and yet it wasn't.'

'I don't think I understand. How do you mean?'

'Well, it was like him. A round face, with heavy lines. Alec was fifteen years older than me. The face had Alec's very small mouth. But it looked like a painting. And the eyes didn't look at me. They stayed half shut. This was how he looked after the doctors had gone. Oh, I was afraid! I put one hand behind me and tried to find the bell. I said, "What does this mean, Alec?" '

Her face was white with fear. She continued:

'Then I got my finger on the bell. He knew this, I could see it. His lips opened and shut, but there was no sound. He was trying to speak. At last he managed to say, "I want you with me!" At that moment the stewardess came to my door,

He was wearing a blue dressing gown and red shoes. That's what he always wore. He was trying to speak. At last he managed to say, 'I want you with me!'

and I did not see him any more.'

'Did you tell the stewardess?'

'Oh, no. I only told her I was afraid of the storm.'

'Mrs Derrison, the explanation is very clear.'

'What is it?' she asked.

'The cause of it was sea-sickness.'

'But I haven't felt ill.'

'Perhaps not. But the brain and body act together. The movement of the boat in a bad storm can hurt the eyes.'

I didn't really know if this was true. But she was very worried, and I had to help her.

'Oh, if I could think that,' she said, 'what a comfort it would be!'

'It won't happen to you again. The weather's getting better.'

She began to tell me her story. She married Alec Derrison nine years ago. She liked him but she wasn't in love with him. But she told him this at the time. He said that it didn't matter. Later she would learn to love him. Well, perhaps many marriages like that become happy ones. But this marriage was a mistake.

Alec took her to his big house in New York. And there they lived for a year. It was all right at first. He was always very kind to her. And he gave her plenty of money. But she still didn't love him. And Alec Derrison began to be afraid he would lose her. He thought she would fall in love with another man.

At the end of the year Alec Derrison took her to England for a holiday. And there she met the man she really loved. He was an artist, the same age as herself.

She went to her husband and told him. And he took her back to New York. He was very kind to her for the eight years until he died. But all the time he watched her. He travelled to England for business reasons every year, but he never took her with him. And while he was away, two of his sisters came to the house, and watched his wife for him.

But somehow she managed to write to the artist. And she received letters from the man she loved all those eight years. And now she was going back to England to marry him.

'You see how it was,' Mrs Derrison said. 'If a dead man could come back again, then certainly Alec would come back. And when you begin to be afraid, the fear grows and grows. He crossed from New York to England more than once in this boat.'

'Well, Mrs Derrison,' I said. 'The dead cannot and don't come back. But a sick person can see strange things, things which aren't really there. There is no reason now why you should be afraid.'

She was much better at lunch, and afterwards. And the next day she seemed quite all right. I believed that the trouble was over.

But it wasn't. On the night before we arrived in Liverpool, I had a talk with Bartlett. He was an old fellow I had met on the boat, and sometimes had a drink with. That evening we had a late drink together, and talked about different subjects. Among these was the power to remember faces.

'Yes, I can remember faces all right,' he said. 'Names trouble me, but not faces. For example, I can remember the faces of the seventy or eighty people in our part of this boat.'

'I thought it was more than that.'

'No, people don't cross the Atlantic in February for pleasure. There aren't more than eighty in this part of the boat. But, you know, it's a funny thing. We've got one man on the boat who never comes out of his room. I saw him for the first time yesterday morning. He was coming out of a bathroom. I've not seen him since. He must hide in his room all the time.'

'He's probably ill.'

'No, not ill. I asked the Doctor. I suppose he doesn't like people.'

'Well, let me see if you can remember. What was he like?'

'That's easy to answer, because he was a bit strange. So he was easy to remember. A man in his fifties, I should say. He wore a blue dressing gown and red shoes. He had something heavy in his pocket. It was a watch, I think. But I noticed his face. It was very round, and the mouth was the smallest I have seen on a man. But the whole look on his face was strange. It seemed like a painting. He walked very slowly, and looked very worried.'

'You can certainly remember people. Have you spoken about him to anybody else?'

'No. Oh, yes, I did mention it to some of the ladies after dinner. Why?'

'I wondered if anybody else saw him.'

'Well, the ladies said no. I've known men like that. They like to be alone.'

A few minutes later I said goodnight to old Bartlett, and

left him. It was between one and two in the morning. His story worried me. I was afraid of meeting something in a blue dressing gown. But I was more afraid about Mrs Derrison. There were very few women on the boat, and it was certain she was in the group which heard his story. I decided to walk past her room.

But before I reached it, the door opened. Mrs Derrison ran out in her night-dress. She had her mouth open. She held one hand to her neck. With the other she held the door shut. She seemed to be trying to hold it shut against somebody. I hurried towards her. She turned and saw me. At once she threw herself into my arms, in fear. She kept saying:

'I've got to go back to him – into the sea, into the sea, into the sea!'

It seemed a long time before she was quiet again and listening to me.

'It was a bad dream,' I said. 'And it's made you afraid, poor child.'

'No, no, not a dream!'

'It didn't seem like one to you. But that's what it was. You're all right now. I'm going to take care of you.'

'Don't leave me for one moment. He wants me with him. He's in my room.'

'Oh no, I'll show you he's not there.'

I opened the door of her room. It was dark inside. I still kept my arm round her.

'I left the light on,' she said in a quiet voice.

'Oh yes,' I said, 'but your arm turned it off as you came out. I saw it.'

This wasn't true, but I could not tell her the truth. I felt like a big brother who was looking after her. She got back into her bed, and I gave her some whisky.

She was still holding my hand.

'Shall I tell you what happened?' she asked.

'Yes, if you like. It was only a dream, you know.'

'I don't think it was a dream. I went to sleep. I didn't think that I would sleep after Mr Bartlett's story. But I did. Then suddenly I awoke. I heard somebody breathing close by my ear. The sound got farther away, and I turned on the light quickly. *He* was standing there. He picked up a small knife from the table. He felt the edge of it, and put it down, shaking his head. Then he moved over to me, and held the side of the bed. "Go into the sea, Sheila," he said quietly. "I'm waiting. I want you. Into the sea." After that I don't know what happened. Suddenly I was holding you. How long ago was it? It doesn't matter. I'm safe while you're here.'

I sat down near her. I said: 'Why are you safe while I'm here?'

'Because you're stronger than he is,' she answered.

I certainly felt that he and I were fighting for her life. And I had got him down. I knew in some strange way that I *was* the stronger.

'Well,' I said, 'the dream of being awake is a very usual one. But what was it Bartlett told you?'

'He said he saw him – in his blue dressing gown and red shoes. He mentioned his small mouth, too.'

'I'm glad you told me that,' I said. What I then told her was not true. I went on:

'The man that Bartlett saw was Curwen. I've just been talking to Bartlett. And he mentioned him to me.'

'Who is Curwen?'

'He's quite a good fellow, an electrical engineer, I believe. Bartlett described him to me.'

'But the colour of his shoes, and ...'

'Oh, that was chance, an unlucky chance for you.'

'I see,' she said. She lay back and rested. I stayed with her till it was light.

I have had the most happy letters from her and from her new husband. I liked the good-looking man who met her at Liverpool. In her letters she speaks of her 'bad dream'. Even now it seems sometimes, she says, that it was real. She sent me an expensive and beautiful gold cigarette case. I cannot use it when I'm with other people. I'm not paid that amount of money! But I like to have it.

Because of my stories about sea-sickness and the engineer Curwen, she has an explanation of what happened. But I myself have no explanation at all. I know this: I could travel to New York by that same boat tomorrow. But I'm waiting three days for another boat.

I have not told you the name of the boat. I do not want to hurt their business. But I believe that boat carries a passenger whose name is not on the passenger list. On every journey. I am sure of it.

2

The Ghost Ship

by Richard Middleton

I live in Fairfield. It's a little village which lies near the Portsmouth Road, about half-way between London and the sea. The year of my story is 1897, when good Queen Victoria still ruled Britain.

Fairfield is an old-fashioned village. It has a village green, an open field of grass, in the middle of it. It has an old church, and an old inn. I know the man who keeps the inn, the landlord, very well.

The other evening I was talking to some Londoners in the inn. They seemed to think the village an uninteresting place. Nothing happened there. Uninteresting! Well, I told them, I've listened to all your stories about London. They don't sound as interesting as the things in Fairfield. We don't talk much about these happenings. We don't tell the world what happens on Saturday nights. But it's then that the ghosts of our young men who died in the war come back. And they meet the girls who now lie dead in the churchyard. We let the ghosts come and go, and don't make any trouble for them. For this reason, Fairfield has more ghosts than any other place in England. I've seen a man without a head sitting on a wall in daylight. There were children playing around his feet as if he was their father. Yes, you can take my word for it. Ghosts know when they are in a good place, just as we do.

But I'm going to tell you about something strange. It was strange, even for this village. It all happened in the spring of 1897. That year we had two great storms. I'll begin with the first one. I remember it well. It lifted the roof of my pigsty, and threw it into the next garden. This belonged to Mrs Lamport. I didn't want to meet her so I went down to the inn and had a drink.

I told the landlord of the inn about it. He laughed. 'Well,' he said, 'the storm has blown something into my field. A kind of ship, I think.'

I was surprised at that. But he said it was only a ghost ship, and would not hurt the vegetables in his field. We argued that the wind had blown it up from the sea at Portsmouth. Then we talked about other things. Part of the roof of the doctor's house was blown down. A big tree came down in Lumley's field. It was an unusually violent storm. About a week later I met the landlord on the village green. He had a worried face. 'That ship in my field is still there. And it's not doing my vegetables any good. My wife will be angry when she sees them.'

So I walked down the country road to his field. And there was the ship in the middle of his field. But it wasn't a modern ship. No. It was about three hundred years old. It was painted black, with lots of fine little figures on it. At the back there was a great window on it, as big as a dining room. There were big old-fashioned guns at little windows in the sides.

'She seems very real for a ghost ship,' I said. The landlord looked worried.

'I don't know what it is,' he answered. 'But it's going to kill our vegetables. My wife won't be very pleased. She'll want it moved.'

We went up to the ship, and touched the side. It was as hard as a real ship.

'Now there are people in England who would say this is very strange,' said the landlord.

Just then we heard a noise on the ship. We looked up and saw a man standing there. He was looking down at us quite peacefully. He was dressed in the clothes of three hundred years ago. His coat was black, edged with gold, and he wore a great sword at his side.

'I'm Captain Bartholomew Roberts,' he said, in a gentleman's voice. 'I've come in to land to find more men. But it seems the ship has come too far.'

'Yes,' cried the landlord, 'you're seventy-five kilometres from the sea.'

'As far as that, is it?' answered Captain Roberts. 'Well, it doesn't matter.'

The landlord was a little angry. 'I don't want to be unneighbourly,' he said, 'but I don't like your ship in my field. You see, my wife likes those vegetables it's on.'

'I'm only here for a few months,' answered the captain quietly. 'Perhaps you will let me send this to your wife.' He took a jewel from his pocket and threw it down to the landlord.

The landlord's face went red. 'My wife likes jewellery,' he

said, 'but this is too much for a few vegetables.' It was a very valuable jewel.

The captain laughed. 'No, sir,' he said. 'you were forced to give up the vegetables, and so you ought to have a good price. Say no more about it. Good-day.' He turned and went into the ship.

The landlord walked back up the road. He wasn't worried now. 'The storm has blown me some luck,' he said. 'My wife will be very pleased with that jewel.'

1897 was a year when many things happened. It was sixty years since Queen Victoria became Queen of England. The people showed their pleasure in many ways. In our village we had great fun, and we hadn't much time to think of other things. The landlord saw the captain once or twice while he was working in his field. And his wife wore the jewel when she went to church on Sundays.

Captain Roberts asked why the church bells were ringing all the time. When he heard about Queen Victoria, he put up a flag on the ship. And he fired off his guns like a good Englishman. The gunshot made a hole in farmer Johnstone's wall. But nobody thought much about it on that happy day.

But when the great day was over we began to notice something wrong in the village. I first heard about it from the shoemaker. He spoke to me one day in the inn. 'You know my great-great-uncle, don't you?' he said.

'You mean Joshua, the quiet young fellow,' I answered. I knew Joshua well.

'*Quiet*!' cried the shoemaker. '*Quiet*! He comes home at three o'clock in the morning, quite drunk. He wakes up the whole house with his noise.'

'It can't be Joshua,' I said. He was one of the quietest ghosts in the village.

'It is Joshua,' answered the shoemaker. 'And one of these nights he'll find himself out in the street, if he isn't careful.'

This kind of talk worried me. I don't like to hear a man talking badly about his family. I could not believe that a quiet young man like Joshua would start drinking too much.

Then a farmer called Alwyn came in. He was very angry and he could hardly drink his beer.

'The young dog! The young dog!' he kept saying. We found out that he was talking about someone in his family. The young man died in battle many hundreds of years ago.

'Drink?' asked the shoemaker. 'Yes,' answered the farmer, 'the young dog!' He emptied his glass.

Well, after that I kept my ears open. It was the same story all over the village. Nearly all the young ghosts of Fairfield were now drinking too much, and coming home drunk in the early hours of the morning. I could hear them when I was in bed. They sang loudly as they passed.

We soon found out where they went to get their drink. The landlord of the inn was angry with the captain of the ghost ship. That's where the drink came from. Nearly every afternoon whisky arrived at the ship, in a great wagon pulled by ghost horses.

One afternoon the priest came to see me. 'I don't like all this drinking,' he said. 'I'm going down to the ship to talk to the captain about it. I want you to come with me.'

I tried to refuse. I said that, after all, they were only a lot of ghosts. So it didn't matter much.

'Dead or alive, I must do something. I must stop this drinking. And you must come with me, John Simmons,' said the priest.

As we got near the ship, I saw the captain. He took his hat off when he saw the priest.

'Sir, I should be glad to have a word with you,' said the priest.

'Come on to the ship, sir, come on to the ship!' cried the captain.

We climbed up, and the captain took us into the room at the back of the ship, where the big window was. It was the most wonderful place you ever saw in your life. It was full of gold and silver plates, jewelled swords, and beautiful chairs. The priest didn't shake his head very hard when the captain brought a silver cup for each of us. He poured us out a drink of whisky.

I drank some of mine, and it changed my feelings about everything. It filled my blood with fire. I've never tasted such whisky. The priest was now talking to the captain about the drinking in the village. But I didn't listen. I looked through the window at the fishes.

The fishes were swimming all over the landlord's vegetables in the field. At the time it seemed the most natural thing in the world. Afterwards, when I thought about it, it seemed to prove it was a ghost ship.

The captain was listening carefully to the priest. When the priest finished, he filled up our cups again.

'I'm sorry to cause trouble anywhere I have been

welcomed,' he said. 'And you will be glad to hear that I shall put out to sea tomorrow night. The boat will leave you then. And now you must wish me a happy journey!'

So we stood up and drank to his success. And that wonderful whisky was like fire in my body.

Then the captain showed us some of the strange things he brought back from far-away countries. I can't remember now what they were. And then I found myself walking across the field with the priest. I was telling him about the fishes I had seen swimming outside the window. He looked at me, and said, 'John Simmons, you should go straight home to bed.'

Well, next day a strong wind began to blow. It blew harder and harder. At about eight o'clock in the evening I heard a loud noise. I looked out into the garden. You won't believe me, but for a second time that year the wind lifted the roof of my pigsty and threw it into Mrs Lamport's garden next door. I didn't wait to hear what she said. I went over to the inn. The wind was very strong. And the landlord had to help me shut the door.

'It's a powerful storm,' he said, handing me the beer. 'There's a big tree down in the old farmer's field.'

'The captain said he would leave tonight,' I said. 'It's a funny thing how these sailors know about the weather.'

'Yes,' said the landlord. 'He goes tonight. He paid us well with the jewel. But it's a good thing he's going. He brings in whisky from London, you know.'

Suddenly the loud noise of the wind stopped. And we couldn't believe our ears. We heard singing! We went to the

Over our heads was the ship that was in the landlord's field all the summer. It was sailing very comfortably through the windy stars.

door and looked out. Over our heads was the ship that was in the landlord's field all the summer. It was sailing very comfortably through the windy stars. All the windows in the ship were lighted, and there was a great sound of singing and music.

'The captain's gone,' cried the landlord. 'And he's taken half the village with him.' I could only move my head in answer. There was so much noise.

In the morning we were able to see the power of the storm. There was enough work to keep the whole village busy for weeks. Roofs were blown away, trees blown down. And we lost many of our ghosts. All the young men sailed with the captain.

It was funny. Those in the village who were most angry about the drinking seemed to miss the ghosts most. And the ghost girls called their lovers by name on the village green at night. It did not seem fair. The poor girls gave up their lives to join them. And now they were alone a second time.

The captain's ship has never come back to Fairfield. But as people grow older they seem to think it will. One of these windy nights the ship will sail in over the field, with all the lost ghosts. Well, when she comes, she'll be welcome. There's one ghost girl that waits and hopes. Every night you'll see her out on the green. She's looking for the lights of the ship among the stars.

The landlord's field wasn't hurt by the visit of the ship. But they do say that, since then, all the vegetables grown in it have tasted of whisky.

3

The Ghost

by Richard Hughes

He killed me quite easily. He banged my head on the stones of the road. *Bang*! God, I was wrong. All my hate went out with that first bang. I was wrong to make all that trouble because I found him with another woman. And now he was doing this to me – *bang*! That was the second one, and with it *everything* went out.

My thin young ghost must have shone a little in the moonlight. I saw him look up from the body in a fixed sort of way. That gave me an idea. I would stay with him. All my life I was afraid of ghosts. Now I was one myself. And so now I would make someone else afraid. *He* was never afraid. He said there weren't such things as ghosts. Oh, weren't there! I'd soon teach him.

John stood up, still looking in front of him. I could see him clearly. Slowly, all my hate came back. I put my face close up against his. But he didn't seem to see it, he just looked in front of him. Then he began to walk forward. He seemed to be going to walk through me. I was afraid. But why should I – a ghost – be afraid of his real body? But fear doesn't act as you would expect, ever. And I moved back before him, and then moved to one side and let him pass. He was almost lost in the dark street before I began to follow him.

But I don't think he could have escaped from me. There was still something between us. It drew me to him whether I wanted it or not. I followed him up to High Street, and then down Long Lane.

Long Lane was full of shadows. But I could still see him as clearly as if it was daylight. Then I felt brave again. I moved more quickly till I was in front of him. Then I turned round, shaking my hands and making an unhappy sound, as the ghosts did in books. He began to smile a little, in a sort of pleased way. But he didn't seem to really see me. Was this because he didn't believe in ghosts? Was this why he couldn't see me?

'*Hoo*!' I cried through my small teeth. '*Hoo*! *Murderer*! *Murderer*!' Someone threw open a top window. 'Who's

Someone threw open a top window. 'Who's that?' she called. 'What's the matter?' So other people could hear me. But I kept silent. I wouldn't tell anyone about him – not yet. And all the time he walked straight forward, smiling to himself. He never had any sense of right and wrong, I said to myself. Here he is with new murder on his mind. And he's smiling easily. But there was a sort of hard look about him.

It was strange. I became a ghost very suddenly. Ten minutes ago I was a living woman. Now I walked on air, with the wind clear and wet against my back. Ha-ha! I laughed loudly, it all seemed so funny. Surely John must have heard *that*. But no, he just turned the corner into Prince Street.

All along Prince Street the trees were losing their leaves. And then I knew what I would do. I made those dead leaves rise up on their thin edges. It looked as if the wind was doing it. All along Prince Street they followed him. They made a sound on the road with their dry edges. But John just walked on through them. And I followed him. As I said, there was still something that held us together.

Only once he turned, and seemed to see me. He almost seemed to recognise me. There was no fear in his face. He looked almost happy. 'You're glad you've killed me,' I thought. 'But you'll be sorry!'

And then all at once the feeling left me. I was only fifteen minutes dead, and I was still thinking of making people pay for their actions. I should in place of this be getting ready to meet my God! A kind of voice in me seemed to say: 'Leave him, Millie, leave him alone *before it is too late!*' Too late? Surely I could leave him when I wanted to? Ghosts follow us as they like, don't they? I'd try just once more to make him afraid. Then I'd stop and think about where I was going in the future.

He stopped, and turned and faced me.

I pointed at him with both my hands.

'John!' I cried. 'John! You needn't stand there and smile, and look at me with your big eyes. You think you've won. But you haven't. I'll *finish* you! I'll …'

I stopped, and laughed a little. Windows were opened. 'Who's that? What's the trouble?' called out the neighbours. They had all heard me. But he only turned and walked on.

'Leave him, Millie, before it's too late,' the voice said

again.

Was that what the voice meant? Leave him before I told the world his secret? To tell it would be a crime. All right, I would, I'd leave him. I'd go straight to meet my God before any accident happened. So I lifted up my two arms. I tried to fly off into the air. But at once some force took hold of me, like a great wind. And I was carried away after him down the street. There was something moving in me still that joined me to him.

It was strange. I was so real to all those people. They thought me still a living woman. But he – who had most reason to fear me – it seemed uncertain that he even saw me. He was going up the deserted length of Prince Street. Where was he going to? He turned into Rock Street. I saw a blue light. That building was the Police Station.

'Oh, God,' I thought, 'I've done it! Oh, God, he's going to tell the police that he did it!'

'You drove him to it,' the voice said. 'Why did you think he didn't see you? What did you think would happen? Did you think he'd cry out and shake with fear at you? Did you think your John wasn't brave? Now his death is on your head!'

'I didn't do it, I didn't!' I cried. 'I never wanted to hurt him, never, not *really*! I wouldn't hurt him, not for anything, I wouldn't. Oh, John, don't look like that! There's still time ... time!'

And all this time he stood in the door, looking at me. The policemen came out and stood round him in a ring. He couldn't escape now.

'That's her,' said one of them in a quiet voice. 'She did it with a heavy piece of iron. Broke his head open. But, God, isn't her face white? She's like someone who's seen a ghost.'

'Oh, John,' I cried. 'I'm sorry. I didn't want to do it! It was because I was angry about that woman ... because I loved you.'

Still the police took no notice of him.

'That's her,' said one of them in a quiet voice. 'She did it with a heavy piece of iron. Broke his head open. But, God, isn't her face white? She's like someone who's seen a ghost.'

'Look at her head, poor girl,' said another policeman. 'She's tried to kill herself with the piece of iron. After she killed him.'

Then the head policeman stepped forward and spoke to me. 'Anything you say will be written down,' he said.

'John!' I cried softly, and held out my arms. Because at last his face softened.

'My God!' said one policeman. 'She's seeing him!'

'They won't kill her,' another said in a quiet voice. 'Did you notice her condition, poor girl?'

4

Jerry Bundler

by W W Jacobs

It was a few days before Christmas. The market town of Torchester was getting ready for the great day. The streets were full of people, but the shops were now closing for the night.

In the old 'Horse-shoe Inn' six travellers were sitting in the comfortable coffee room. There was a good fire burning, and they sat and talked by the light of it. Most of them were businessmen, and at first they talked about business. Then the conversation moved from business to wider subjects, and then, at last, to ghosts.

Three ghost stories were told, but no one seemed very interested. There was too much noise outside the inn, and too much light inside the room. But the fourth story had more success. The streets were now quiet, and the storyteller turned off the gas lights first so the firelight shone on the glasses, and danced with the shadows on the walls. This story held the interest of the listeners.

'I call that a good story,' said one of the men, drinking his hot whisky. 'Of course, it's an old idea that ghosts like to be with human beings. A man told me once about a ghost in the train. He was travelling in a train with a ghost, and didn't know it at first. Then the railway man came in to take the tickets. The ghost seemed to be looking in his pockets for his ticket for a long time. Then it stopped looking, gave a little cry, and disappeared through the window.'

'That's enough, Hirst,' said another man.

'But it's not a subject for joking,' said a little old gentleman. 'I've never seen a ghost myself. But I know people who have. In fact there's a ghost story about this house, you know.'

'I've never heard of it,' said another speaker, 'and I've been here some years now.'

'It goes back a long time now,' said the old gentleman. He spoke to the old waiter, who came in. 'George, you've heard the story about Jerry Bundler, haven't you?'

'Well, I've heard a little, sir,' answered the old waiter, 'but I didn't really believe it. There was one fellow working here who saw it. Or said that he saw it. The manager told him to leave the inn.'

'Well,' said the old gentleman, 'my father was born in this town. He knew the story well. And he was a truthful man and a churchgoer. He saw the ghost of Jerry Bundler in this inn. He told me that.'

'And who was this Bundler?' asked a voice.

'A London thief, a criminal,' answered the old gentleman. 'And he was caught here one Christmas week, about eighty years ago. He had his last supper in this room. And after he went to bed, two policemen arrived. They followed him from London. They went up the stairs to his room with the landlord. They tried to open the door. It was very strong, and they couldn't open it. So one of the policemen went down to the street. He climbed up to the window of the room where Jerry Bundler was. The people in the street looked up and saw the thief at the window. Then there was the noise of breaking glass. The policeman fell from the window to the stones at their feet. Then in the moonlight they saw the white face of the thief, still at the window.'

'The other policeman, with the landlord, was trying to break down the door of the room. There was heavy furniture inside, but at last they got into the room. And the first thing they saw was the body of Jerry Bundler. It was hanging from the top of the bed by his own handkerchief.'

'Which bedroom was it?' asked a voice.

The storyteller shook his head. 'That I can't tell you. But the story goes that Jerry is still seen in this house. He tries to kill people but never succeeds.'

'That doesn't make sense,' said the old gentleman, rising. 'But ghosts can't hurt you, of course. I should quite like to see one. Goodnight, gentlemen.'

'Goodnight,' said the others.

'Shall I light the gas, Mr Malcolm?' asked George, the waiter.

'No, the fire gives enough light,' said the traveller. 'Now, gentlemen, do any of you know any more ghost stories?'

'I think we've had enough ghost stories for one night,' said another man. 'We're not all like the old gentleman that's just gone.'

But Hirst said, 'I should like to try the old gentleman out. Suppose I dress like Jerry Bundler, and go and give him a chance to show his bravery?'

'Good!' said Malcolm. 'No!' said the others.

'Just for the joke, gentlemen,' said Hirst.

'No, no! Drop it, Hirst,' said the others.

'Only for the joke,' said Hirst. 'I've got some old-fashioned clothes in my room. I'm going to be an actor in a play. I have to wear the sort of clothes they wore in Jerry Bundler's time, eighty years ago. I'm a good actor, aren't I, Somers?'

'Oh, you're all right!' said his friend with a laugh.

'I'll pay you a pound if you make me afraid,' said Malcolm.

'All right,' answered Hirst. 'If I don't *I'll* pay *you* the money.'

'You won't make us afraid,' said another man, 'because we're ready for you. But you mustn't try it on the old gentleman. It's dangerous.'

'Well, I'll try you first,' said Hirst, jumping up. 'Don't light the gas.'

They went on talking after he left the room. Two of the travellers went to bed. It was getting late. After half an hour, George ran into the room.

'He's coming, gentlemen!' he cried. 'I saw him in the bar. There wasn't much light there.'

'I'll go and bring him in,' said Malcolm.

'No, no, you don't know what it's like, sir!' said George, holding him back.

Suddenly there was a cry from outside the room, and someone ran towards the door and into the room.

'What is it? What's the matter?' asked Malcolm. 'Oh, it's

Mr Hirst!'

'Light the gas, George,' said Malcolm.

The waiter lit it. They could now see Hirst clearly. He was dressed in the old-fashioned clothes. But he hadn't had time to finish dressing. And he was still shaking with fear.

'Now, what's the matter?' asked Malcolm.

'I've seen the ghost,' said Hirst breathlessly, 'I'll never make a joke about it again, never!'

He looked through the open door of the room.

'I thought I saw it again. Look – can you see anything?'

'No, there's nothing there,' said Malcolm. But his own voice shook a little. 'Go on.'

'I turned round and saw it,' continued Hirst. 'It had a white, dead face.'

'That's what I saw in the bar,' said George. 'Fearful, it was.'

Hirst dropped into a chair, shaking with fear.

'Well, this is a very strange thing,' said Malcolm, turning to the others. 'It's the last time I come to this inn.'

'I leave tomorrow,' said George the waiter. 'I won't go down to that bar again myself, no, not for fifty pounds.'

'It's because we've been talking about it. That's made it happen,' said one of the men.

'It's strange that George and Hirst *both* think they saw something,' said Malcolm. 'I'm half afraid to go up to bed.'

'I saw it as clearly as I see you, sir,' said George. He pointed out of the open door. They followed the direction of his finger with their eyes, but saw nothing. One of them thought a head looked round the corner of the wall, but he wasn't certain. Malcolm went out of the room in the direction of the bar, but then came back into the room.

'Did you see it, sir?' asked George.

'I don't know,' said Malcolm quietly. 'How are you feeling now?' he asked Hirst.

'Oh, I feel better now,' answered Hirst. He spoke coldly. Everyone was looking at him.

'Perhaps you think I'm not very brave,' he said. 'But you didn't see it.'

Malcolm said, smiling a little, 'Not at all.'

'I'm going to bed,' said Hirst, noticing the smile. 'Will you sleep in my room, Somers?'

'Certainly,' said his friend, 'if you'll keep the gas lighted all night.'

Hirst and Somers left and went up to their room. The others heard their door close.

'Well,' said Malcolm, standing in front of the fire. 'I suppose I must pay Hirst a pound. But really, I think I won. I never saw a man so afraid in all my life.'

'Will someone sleep in my room?' asked one of his listeners. 'I'm afraid to be alone.'

'I will,' said Malcolm.

'And I suppose we're together, Mr Leek,' said a third man, turning to the fourth man there.

'No, thank you,' answered Leek. 'I don't believe in ghosts. If anything comes into my room, I'll shoot it with my gun.'

'That won't hurt a ghost, Leek,' said Malcolm.

'Well, the noise will wake the house,' answered Leek.

'But if you're afraid, sir,' he said to the third man, 'George will sleep inside your door, I'm sure.'

'Yes, I will, sir,' said George. 'And please could you gentlemen come down with me to the bar? I have to put the gas out.'

They all went out together, except Leek. They looked carefully in front of them as they went. George turned out the light in the bar, and they returned safely to the coffee room. They then got ready to go to their rooms.

'Give me the light while you put the gas out, George,' said Malcolm.

The waiter handed the light to him, and turned off the gas. At that moment they all heard a noise. It was the sound of someone outside the door. Then the door of the coffee room opened slowly. Malcolm fell back with his mouth open. A white face appeared at the door. The eyes were set deep in the head.

For a few seconds the figure stood looking at them. Then it came a little way into the room and stood there.

Not a man spoke or moved. They all watched the figure. It took off something from its neck, and then its head fell sideways. The figure stood still. Then it moved towards Malcolm, holding something out in front of it.

There was a loud bang, and the light went out. They could see something lying on the floor. There was noisy breathing, and then silence.

Malcolm was the first to speak. 'Matches,' he said in a strange voice. George lighted a match. Then he lighted the gas. Malcolm touched the thing on the floor with his foot,

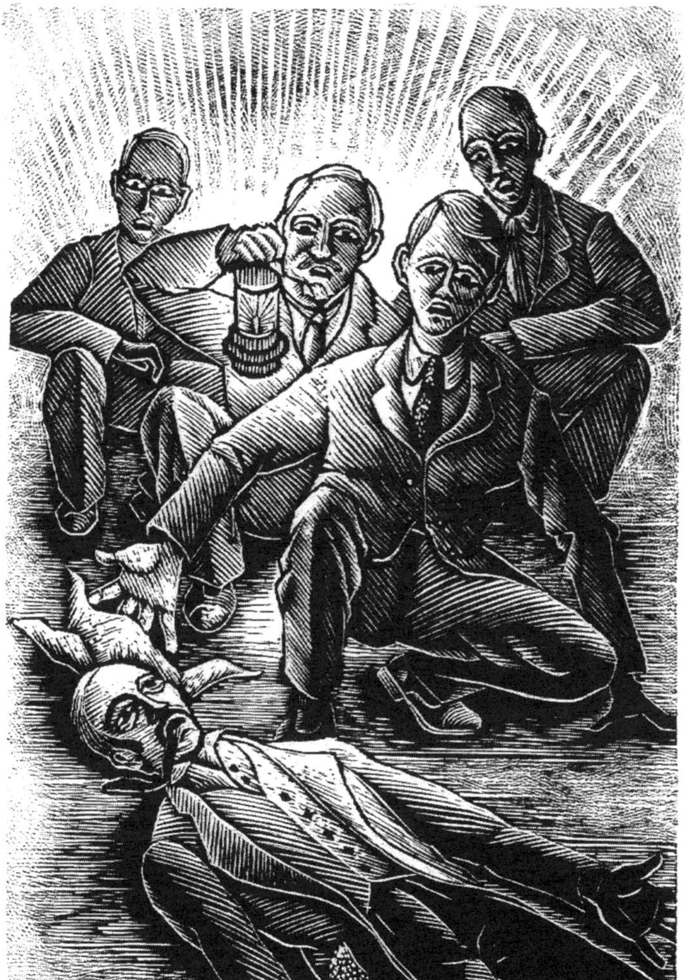

He wetted his handkerchief, and with it cleaned the white face. He fell back with a cry of fear, looking at the face.

and found it soft. He looked at the other men. They were trying to ask him a question, but he shook his head. He brought a light nearer, and bending down, looked closely at the silent thing on the floor.

Then he got up quickly, and brought some water from the table. He wetted his handkerchief, and with it cleaned the white face. He fell back with a cry of fear, looking at the face. Leek's gun fell to the floor and he shut out the sight of the dead man with both hands. The others came forward and looked fearfully at the dead face of Hirst.

Before a word was spoken, the door opened. Somers came in quickly. His eyes were wide with fear as he looked at the dead man.

'Good God!' he cried, 'You didn't ...'

Nobody spoke.

'I told him not to,' he said in a weak voice. 'I told him not to. I told him ...'

He looked deathly sick. He put his arms out weakly, and fell senseless into the arms of Malcolm.

5

Over a Whisky Bottle

by WC Morrow

It happened about a hundred years ago in the city of San Francisco. Arthur Kimberlin was a young man in great trouble. He was a stranger in the city, with no work and no money to buy food. He could not steal. But he was now weak with hunger. His last meal was seventy hours ago. It was cold, dark, and raining. He went for comfort to the streets where the restaurants were. There he could smell the food which he couldn't buy.

In Mason Street he stopped outside a restaurant with a lot of food in the window. By now his hunger really hurt him. A little farther on there was another restaurant which had a bar. One of its doors had the words 'Family entrance' on it. Just inside this door stood a man, looking straight out into the street. There was something in the man's face which made Kimberlin stop. He looked hard at the stranger. The man's face was white, and his eyes were still fixed on the street in front of him. Then he noticed young Kimberlin.

'Ah,' he said, 'the rain has caught you too. And you haven't got an overcoat. Stand in this doorway. There's room for two.'

The voice was hard, but not unkind. And they were the

first words anyone spoke to Kimberlin in that city. The two men stood in the doorway for a little time in silence. Then the stranger said:

'It may rain for some time. I'm cold, and I notice that you're shaking with cold. Let us step inside and get a drink.'

He opened the door, and Kimberlin followed. Hope began to lay a warm hand on his heart. The stranger led the way into one of the little open rooms or compartments where people sat to drink together at a table. Before the stranger sat down he put his hand into his pocket. He pulled out a number of bank notes.

'You're younger than I am,' he said. 'Will you go to the bar and buy a bottle of whisky. And bring some water and some glasses. Here's a twenty dollar note.'

Kimberlin took the note and started off in the direction of the bar. He held the money in his hand. It felt warm and comfortable. How many lovely hot meals could that note buy! He held it harder. He looked back at the door of the compartment where the stranger was. It was closed. He could pass it, leave the restaurant, run away and buy himself a good meal somewhere else. For a moment he thought he would do it. Then he turned round again, and walked straight to the bar. He gave the order to the barman.

'You aren't going to drink all of that, are you?' asked the barman.

'I have friends in the box,' answered Kimberlin. 'We want to drink quietly by ourselves. We're in box number 7.'

'Oh, I'm sorry. That's all right,' said the barman.

Kimberlin's step was much stronger as he returned with the

drink. He opened the door of the compartment, number 7. The stranger was waiting at the side of the little table. He was looking at the wall in front of him, in a fixed way. He wore a wide hat, pulled well down. He didn't seem to notice Kimberlin at first. Kimberlin put the bottle and glasses and the water on the table, and sat down in front of the stranger. Then he noticed Kimberlin.

'Oh, you have brought it,' he said. 'How kind of you. Now please fasten the door.'

Kimberlin took the change from the note from his pocket. But the stranger said:

'Keep the change. You'll need it. I'm going to get it back in a way that might interest you. Let us first drink, and then I'll explain.'

They drank, and the whisky began to warm Kimberlin. 'It will do us good,' said the stranger. 'Now, do you know how to play dice?'

Kimberlin didn't. He knew of course that games of chance were played with these pieces with the numbers one to six on the sides.

'I thought not. Well, please go to the bar and bring a dice box. I won't ring for it. I don't want the waiter here.'

Kimberlin brought the box, and again fastened the door of the little room. The game then began. It was not one of the easy old games, but much more difficult. And brains as well as chance played a part. After a game or two, the stranger said:

'You seem to understand it now. Well, I'll show you that you don't. Now we'll throw for a dollar a game. In that way

They drank, and the whisky began to warm Kimberlin. 'It will do us good,' said the stranger. 'Now, do you know how to play dice?'

I shall win the money that you received in change.'

'I shall enjoy the game,' answered Kimberlin.

'Let's have another drink before we start. I believe I'm growing colder.'

They drank again, and the hungry young man enjoyed his drink. It warmed his whole body, and he almost forgot his hunger.

They played for a dollar a game. Kimberlin won. The stranger smiled and opened another game. Again Kimberlin won. Then the stranger pushed back his hat and fixed his eyes on the young man. He was still smiling. But when Kimberlin looked at him, he felt afraid. The stranger's face was very white, as white as death.

Kimberlin's mind was made clearer by the whisky. He noticed the deep lines on the stranger's face, which the electric light brought out very clearly. The face might have been cut in stone. The eyes were black, with a heavy look. The hands were white and thin. As Kimberlin looked, the stranger pulled down his hat.

'You're lucky,' he said. 'Suppose we try another drink. Whisky helps the brain. I see that you and I are going to have a good game.'

After the drink, the game continued. Kimberlin won nearly every game. It was very exciting. His eyes shone. Colour came to his face. The stranger brought out more dollar bills, several thousand of them. They put more money on the games. At Kimberlin's right hand were his winnings – about two hundred dollars. Chance turned the stranger's way, and he won easily for a while. Then it moved back to

Kimberlin's side.

By this time the whisky made Kimberlin's brain very clear, and his hunger now began to return with greater force. Couldn't he order a supper with what he now had? No, that was impossible. The stranger said nothing about eating. Kimberlin went on playing, but he jumped sometimes when the hunger took him. The stranger didn't seem to notice. They did not speak, but they sometimes drank. The money at Kimberlin's right hand grew more and more.

Then the man began to act strangely. At times he threw back his head and listened carefully. Then he returned to his game. Kimberlin thought he was becoming more tired and slow. When Kimberlin won, the stranger fixed his eyes on him and this made him afraid.

But then the stranger brought out more dollar notes of high value. They now played for a thousand dollars a game, and still Kimberlin was winning. At last the stranger said in a low, quiet voice:

'You've won seventy-four thousand dollars. That's exactly the same amount as I have left. We have played for several hours, and I am tired, and I suppose you are. Let's finish the game. Each will now put everything he has, and throw a last dice for it.'

Kimberlin agreed. He threw the dice, and the two men looked at the numbers. This set of numbers was unusually good. Could the stranger do better? Could he throw a better set of numbers? The stranger did not hurry. He took a long time before he threw. And he won.

The stranger sat and looked at the dice on the table for a

long time. Then he lifted his eyes to look at Kimberlin's face, and he didn't say a word. One cannot keep one's eyes open very long without moving them, but the stranger did.

Kimberlin began to feel uncomfortable. 'I'll go now,' he said to the stranger. But he had no money and was in great need of food.

The stranger did not answer, and did not move his eyes from Kimberlin's face. The young man sat back in his own chair, very much afraid. Then he heard two men talking in the next compartment. One said:

'Yes, he was seen to turn into this street. It was about four hours ago.'

'Perhaps it wasn't him.'

'Well, the description of the man they saw fits him. They noticed this strange white face. He isn't well – he has heart disease.'

'He's a clever thief. This is the largest amount of money ever stolen from a bank here. A hundred and forty-eight thousand dollars – think of it! How long is it since he came out of prison?'

'Eight years. In that time he's lived by dice-throwing. People think they can find out how he always wins. But that's impossible. No one ever wins a game with him. But it's clear he isn't in this place. Let's look for him somewhere else.'

The two men left the next compartment, and went out into the street. The two dice players – the white-faced one, and the hungry young man – sat looking at each other. There were a hundred and forty-eight thousand dollars lying on the table between them. The winner made no move to take the money. He just sat and looked at Kimberlin, unmoved by the conversation in the next room.

Kimberlin began to shake with cold. The continuing look of the stranger sent ice into his bones. He moved to one side. Then he discovered the truth. The eyes of the stranger did not follow him. They continued to look straight at the wall in front. A great fear took hold of Kimberlin. He thought people were talking quietly outside the little room. He drank some more whisky, watching the stranger. The whisky seemed to make his heart jump, and he couldn't breathe. His hunger seemed now to be eating him up. He spoke to the stranger, but there was no answer. One of the man's hands lay on the table. He placed one of his own hands on it. Then he moved back in fear. The stranger's hand was as cold as stone.

The money could not be left there. Kimberlin put it together, watching the stranger closely as he did this. *He was afraid he might move!* Kimberlin sat at his own seat at the table, in front of the stranger. And so the two sat and looked at each other. Kimberlin began to breathe more heavily. But his heart did not seem to move so fast. He felt more comfortable, and quite sleepy.

Suddenly a strong light seemed to break on him. He jumped up. Had he been banged on the head, or cut to the heart? No, he was alive. The stranger still sat there, looking at nothing, not moving. But Kimberlin wasn't afraid of him now. He didn't feel weak and afraid now. He felt brave, and able to decide things. Quickly he picked up the money and put it in his pockets.

'Why should I be hungry,' he said to himself, 'with all this money here?'

He carefully unfastened the door of the little room, stepped out, and closed it again. Then, without any fear, he walked out into the street. He was surprised to see the city full of people, and very busy. It was early evening, but the sky was clear. So he wasn't in the restaurant very long, he thought. He walked along the street, feeling lighter than air, and not thinking about the danger he was in. He laughed softly and happily, thinking of all the food he could buy and eat now. He decided to feed all the hungry people without charging them any money. How wonderful it was to be able to buy food, after three days and nights without it! But the poor fellow didn't go and get food.

Never before in his life did he walk with such ease and lightness. His feet did not seem to touch the ground. He felt he was growing bigger and taller. The people he met seemed very small. The streets got wider. The stars became suns, and electric lights became weak. The most wonderful smells and the sweetest music filled the air. Laughing and singing, Kimberlin joined in the sound of music that moved over the city. And then ...

Two policemen were in the restaurant in Mason Street. They were the two men Kimberlin heard talking in the next compartment. They left the restaurant, but after a time they returned. They found the door of room number 7 fastened. They broke open the door, and there they saw two men. One was of middle age, and the other very young.

They were sitting quite still. In the strangest way they were looking straight at each other across the table. Between them was a great amount of money, lying on the table. There was also an empty whisky bottle and a dice box. The dice lay before the older man.

One of the policemen pointed his gun at the older man and ordered:

'Put up your hands!'

But the dice thrower took no notice. The policemen looked at each other. Then they moved nearer to the two men. They looked more closely at their faces. And they discovered that both were dead.

Exercises

A Comprehension

NOT ON THE PASSENGER LIST

Try to remember. Then check your answers.

1 What was the weather like when the story began?
2 Why was Mrs Derrison going to England?
3 What was the terrible act the ghost of Alec Derrison told Mrs Derrison to do?
4 How did the narrator* explain the ghost to Mrs Derrison?
5 Did the narrator believe that there was a ghost on board the ship?

* NOTE: A **narrator** is a person who tells the story

THE GHOST SHIP

Are these statements true or false? Check your answers.

	True	*False*
1 John Simmons, the narrator of the story, comes from London.	□	□
2 The ship that landed in the landlord's field was a modern ocean liner.	□	□
3 To pay the landlord for destroying his vegetables, the captain gave him a jewel for his wife.	□	□
4 The priest was angry at the captain for getting all the ghosts drunk.	□	□
5 Many of the villagers left Fairfield on the ghost ship.	□	□

THE GHOST

Try to remember. Then check your answers.

1 Why did Millie say that her lover, John, killed her?
2 What warning did the 'voice' give Millie?
3 Who did the police arrest and why?
4 Who was the ghost and why did the ghost go to the Police Station?
5 What do you think Millie's *condition* was?

JERRY BUNDLER

Choose the right answer, A, B or C. Then check your answers.

1 The six travellers in the coffee room told stories about …
   A the old 'Horse-shoe Inn'
   B ghosts
   C the war
2 When Jerry Bundler was alive, he was a(n) …
   A storyteller
   B innkeeper
   C thief
3 The only traveller who wanted Hirst to dress up as a ghost was …
   A Malcolm
   B Leek
   C Somers
4 The two men who said they saw the ghost of Jerry Bundler were …
   A Leek and Hirst
   B Malcolm and George
   C Hirst and George
5 Leek shot Hirst because he thought …
   A Hirst was going to attack him
   B Hirst was a ghost
   C someone was trying to rob the travellers

OVER A WHISKY BOTTLE

Try to remember. Then check your answers.

1 What are the three things the reader is told about Arthur Kimberlin at the beginning of the story?
2 What did Arthur Kimberlin want to do when the stranger gave him a twenty dollar note to buy a bottle of whisky?
3 What does the stranger want to do when Arthur Kimberlin returns with a bottle of whisky?
4 What are the two men in the next compartment discussing?
5 What does Arthur Kimberlin realise when he looks at the stranger for the last time?
6 What does the reader realise about Arthur Kimberlin at the end of the story?

B Language Skills

1 WORD BUILDING

Make nouns from the words in brackets to fill the gaps, as in the example.

Example: But he was now weak with hunger. (*hungry*)

1 'I don't like all this .... ,' said the priest. (*drink*)
2 But the fourth story had more .... (*successfully*)
3 They followed the .... of his finger with their eyes, but saw nothing. (*direct*)
4 It's not a subject for .... (*joke*)
5 'Well, the .... of the man they saw fits him.' (*describe*)

2 WORD SEARCH

The five words, 1–5, have all appeared in *Five Ghost Stories*.

Choose the right word, A, B or C, to complete these sentences.

1 A *bang* is ...
  A a loud noise
  B a group of people
  C a seat
2 Something which is *impossible* ...
  A can happen
  B could happen
  C can't happen
3 A person who is *brave* is ...
  A fearful
  B afraid
  C fearless
4 An *actor* is someone ...
  A who acts in plays
  B who works with money
  C who arrests people
5 *Lighted* means the same as ...
  A matched
  B lit
  C fired

C Activities

WRITING

1 Whilst staying in an old farmhouse in the country on a dark and windy night, you saw a ghost. Write and tell a friend about your experience.
2 Write a short paragraph of no more than 75 words saying what you think makes a 'scary' ghost story. You should use

the five ghost stories in your book as examples of what you mean.

3 Look again at the story *The Ghost*. In no more than 50 words, explain what you think happened to Millie and John before the story began.

DISCUSSION

1 Why do you think that some people believe in ghosts while other people do not?

2 What reasons do people who don't believe in ghosts give to explain them?

Glossary

accident
an unfortunate happening i.e. car accident

dressing gown
a type of coat worn indoors before a person dresses

drunk
result of drinking too much alcohol

electrical engineer
a person who is skilled in dealing with machines run by electricity

explanation
something said that makes things clear or plain

Hope began to lay a warm hand on his heart
he began to have hope

jewel
a valuable stone i.e. a diamond

murder
killing

narrator
a person who tells a story

not right in the head
mad, crazy

old-fashioned
not modern, to do with style and/or values of the past

pigsty
a place on a farm where you keep pigs

sea-sick
made sick by the movement of a ship at sea

senseless
without feeling of mind or body

steward/stewardess
a man/woman who looks after people on a ship (or plane)

subject
a person or matter being talked or written about
uncomfortable
not feeling relaxed in body or mind
unmoved
not taking any notice of something; not caring
unneighbourly
acting as a bad neighbour would
whisky
a strong alcoholic drink often made in Scotland or Ireland
without charging them any money
free

Longman English Library

Series editor: Lewis Jones

A library of graded readers for students of English as a foreign language, and for reluctant native readers. The books are graded in six levels of difficulty.

Structure, vocabulary, idiom and sentence length are all controlled. Level 1 has a basic vocabulary of 300 words and appropriate structures, 2: 600 words, 3: 1000 words, 4: 1500 words, 5: 2000 words and 6: 2500 words. Those titles which are asterisked are accompanied by a cassette.

Level Three

David Copperfield* *Charles Dickens*
Five Ghost Stories* *Viola Huggins*
An American Tragedy *Theodore Dreiser*
Six American Stories* *N Wymer*
The Picture of Dorian Gray* *Oscar Wilde*
A Room with a View *E M Forster*
The Importance of Being Earnest *Oscar Wilde*